A Catfish Tale

A Bayou Story of the Fisherman and His Wife

Whitney Stewart

www.av2books.com

Illustrations by
Gerald Guerlais

Your AV² Media Enhanced book gives you a fiction readalong online. Log on to www.av2books.com and enter the unique book code from this page to use your readalong.

AV² Readalong Navigation

Go to **www.av2books.com**, and enter this book's unique code.

BOOK CODE

N971688

AV² by Weigl brings you media enhanced books that support active learning.

First Published by

ALBERT WHITMAN & COMPANY

Publishing children's books since 1919

HIGHLIGHTED TEXT

START READING

PAGE TURNING

HOME

CLOSE

TITLE INFORMATION

PAGE PREVIEW

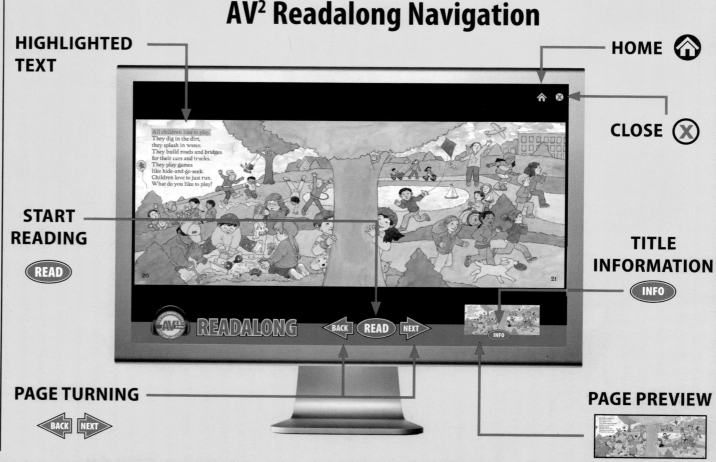

Published by AV² by Weigl
350 5th Avenue, 59th Floor New York, NY 10118
Websites: www.av2books.com   www.weigl.com

Library of Congress Control Number: 2014937155

ISBN 978-1-4896-2840-4 (hardcover)
ISBN 978-1-4896-2841-1 (single user eBook)
ISBN 978-1-4896-2842-8 (multi-user eBook)

Printed in the United States of America in North Mankato, Minnesota
1 2 3 4 5 6 7 8 9 0 18 17 16 15 14

042014
WEP080414

Text copyright ©2014 by Whitney Stewart.
Illustrations copyright ©2014 by Albert Whitman & Company.
Published in 2014 by Albert Whitman & Company.

You ever heard the story of the fisherman and his wife? It's an old tale my pawpaw told me when I was just a hatchling. Some say it's a lie, but Pawpaw swore he saw it all happen with his own eyes.

A sweet young couple named Jacques and Jolie lived way on down the bayou. Jacques liked to pole his skiff through cypress knees to his favorite fishing hole. And Jolie peppered seafood gumbo so hot it made her husband's head sweat.

Each night that woman sang so true,
even the cicadas hushed up to listen.

5

One day Jacques's fishing pole
started bending and shaking. He
grabbed a hold and pulled so hard
that a catfish sprang from the water.

"Hold on there," the catfish cried.
"Don't be thinkin' 'bout supper when
you look at me. I'm a magic catfish,
and I'd spoil your gumbo pot."

Jacques never did hear a catfish talk
before and it gave him a fright. So
he freed that jabbering critter and
paddled home for the night.

"You did WHAT?!" Jolie hollered when Jacques told his catfish tale. "You didn't ask for even one small wish?"

Jacques looked around and scratched his head. "What could I have wished for, *ma chère*? I don't need nothin' more."

8

Jolie's face turned crawfish red. "Do you have eyes inside your head? This shack is sinking in the mud. Go ask for a proper house where I can sing to a crowd."

Jacques paddled back out to
the swamp to beg that catfish
to show his whiskers again.
And he asked for Jolie's house.

The catfish just grinned and said, "Ah, tooloulou—if that ain't the easiest thing to do."

Jacques had never seen a house so big, but Jolie filled it with friends and sang through the night.

At breakfast she announced, "I'm going to take my show on the road. All I need is a paddle wheel boat. Go ask that catfish for one more little thing."

Jacques thought Jolie was asking for too much.
But the catfish liked this fisherman. He smiled real wide and said, "Ah, tooloulou—if that ain't the easiest thing to do."

Jolie stood at the bow of her boat and sang to her fans. Up and down the river, they called her *Queen of the Mississippi*. Jolie loved being queen.

Poor Jacques huddled in a cabin with an aching head. All that carrying-on was too much for him. And he missed his fishing pole. So back he went to the bayou to find his catfish friend.

Jolie filled the nightclubs of New Orleans. Her name was on the front page of every newspaper.

Mardi Gras season was coming soon. People loved the parades.

"I want to be queen of Mardi Gras," Jolie wrote to Jacques. "Go ask that catfish for one more little thing."

Jacques found the catfish in the same old place, and he asked his new *ami*, "Could Jolie have just one more wish?"

And this was his friend's reply, "Ah, tooloulou—if that ain't the easiest thing to do."

Jolie wore a diamond crown and a white satin gown. She rode on a float past cheering crowds, but nobody could hear her sing. She tried to throw out Mardi Gras beads and tangled them in her crown. But oh how she loved being queen.

When carnival was over, she missed her royal robes. So she wrote her husband again and said, "I want to be Queen of the Bayou. Go ask that catfish for one more little thing."

Now this was just too much.

But Jacques asked the catfish anyway. And you know what that catfish said?

"Ah, tooloulou—if that ain't the easiest thing to do."

In a spectacle that outshined the sun, pelicans crowned Jolie queen. She stepped onto the stage, and her fans applauded. Musicians blared their horns. Jolie cleared her throat, closed her eyes, took a deep breath, and began to sing.

All at once the winds started to howl and black clouds filled the sky.

Trees twisted and turned and fish jumped from the river. Jolie's voice stirred up a hurricane and people ran for cover.

Thunder boomed and lightning struck the church steeple. Snakes, alligators, and swamp creatures slithered up the riverbank. Ghosts and goblins flew from the cemeteries and pirate skeletons escaped watery graves to dance in the streets.

The storm sped across the stage, swooped Jolie up, and spun her through the sky…

25

And into the treetops.

Jolie hung on a branch like a crumpled doll. She sang out an urgent message to a passing pelican, "I've had enough of being queen! Tell my husband to ask that catfish for ONE MORE LITTLE THING!"

Jacques paddled faster than an alligator could swish its tale. He begged the catfish for one last wish. He meant it—really—*one last wish.* And what do you think the catfish said? Hmm?

Nope. You'd be wrong.
He just winked at Jacques and disappeared 'neath the water.

'Cause Jolie didn't need nothin' more.

Bayou Glossary

ami—friend

bayou—small river or creek that runs through lowland

cher—dear (*mon cher* means "my dear" referring to a boy, while *ma chère* refers to a girl)

cicada—insect found in temperate to tropical climate that makes a buzzing sound

crawfish—small, lobsterlike crustacean

gumbo—soup or stew, common in the South

pawpaw—grandfather

tooloulou—fiddler crab

Mardi Gras—carnival with parades, costumes, parties, and colorful beads

Seafood Gumbo Recipe

Recipe by   Hans Andersson, New Orleans native

Start with a roux:

4 tbsp salted butter   1 cup flour

Melt butter in a heavy pot, and add the flour. Stir the roux continuously over medium heat to prevent burning. (If the roux begins to smoke, it is too hot; reduce heat.) Keep stirring for 20–30 minutes until the roux is dark brown.

Make the gumbo:

5 cups fish stock*
1 cup onion, finely diced
1 clove garlic, minced
1 bay leaf
3 celery stalks
2–4 oz. stewed tomatoes

10–15 raw shrimp, peeled
4 oz. oysters, with oyster "liquor" (the natural liquid from shucked oysters), set aside
4 oz. crab meat

Add the onions, garlic, and celery to the pot with the roux, and sauté for 3–5 minutes until vegetables are lightly browned. Slowly add small amounts of fish stock, and mix well to avoid clumping the roux. When the roux is blended smoothly with the liquid, add the remaining stock, then add stewed tomatoes and oyster liquor; stir for 5 minutes. Add shrimp, oysters, and crabmeat.
Simmer for 30 minutes, and add bay leaf, cayenne pepper, and salt to taste. Serve in bowls over rice. Serves 6 to 8.

*For truly authentic gumbo, start with homemade fish stock made with white fish and shrimp.